We Fell Apart, And I Wrote About It.

Disha Agarwal

Ukiyoto Publishing

All global publishing rights are held by

Ukiyoto Publishing

Published in 2025

Content Copyright © Disha Agarwal

ISBN 9789370099920

All rights reserved.

No part of this publication may be reproduced, transmitted, or stored in a retrieval system, in any form by any means, electronic, mechanical, photocopying, recording or otherwise, without the prior permission of the publisher.

The moral rights of the author have been asserted.

This is a work of fiction. Names, characters, businesses, places, events, locales, and incidents are either the products of the author's imagination or used in a fictitious manner. Any resemblance to actual persons, living or dead, or actual events is purely coincidental.

This book is sold subject to the condition that it shall not by way of trade or otherwise, be lent, resold, hired out or otherwise circulated, without the publisher's prior consent, in any form of binding or cover other than that in which it is published.

www.ukiyoto.com

To The Ones Who Leave, And The Ones Who Stay

There are certain heartbreaks that don't shatter us all at once — they break us slowly, in moments of silence, in words left unsaid, and in memories that cling to our skin long after the people are gone.

This is an anthology for those who loved too deeply and lost too painfully.

For the ones who gave too much.

For the ones who stayed when the other was already gone.

In these pages, I have poured the weight of what it feels like to lose not just love, but a piece of yourself in the process. Through poetry and letters, I have written the story of breaking and becoming — the love, the falling apart, and the healing that followed.

If you've ever loved someone who couldn't stay,

This is for you.

Contents

Section I: The Beginning (Where Love Felt Infinite)   1
"When We Were Infinite"   3
Sonnet: "In the Glow of What We Were"   4
Haiku: "Shattered Bonds"   5
Narrative Poetry: "The Bridge We Burned"   6
"Before the Fall"   7
"I Was Yours Before I Knew Myself"   8
Letter: "When Love Was Still Ours"   9

Section II: The Falling Apart (Where Everything We Built Collapsed)   11
The Silence Between Us"   13
Sonnet: "The Day You Stopped Saying My Name"   14
Haiku: "Falling Out of Us"   15
Prose Poetry: "The Night We Broke Without Words"   16
Lyrical Poetry: "You Let Me Go So Easily"   17
Narrative poetry: "The Stranger You Became"   18
Letter: "The Breaking That Became Me"   19

Section III: The Aftermath (Where I Learned To Survive)   21
"I Loved You and I Survived"   23
Sonnet - "What Healing Sounds Like"   24
Haiku: "I Let You Go"   25
Prose Poetry: "The Day I Stopped Waiting for You"   26
Lyrical Poetry: "I Loved, I Lost, I Grew"   27

Narrative Poetry: "The Version of Me That No Longer
Loves You" 28

Final Letter: "To The Version of Me That Survived" 29

About the Author *31*

Section I: The Beginning (Where Love Felt Infinite)

We Fell Apart, And I Wrote About It.

"When We Were Infinite"

We ran barefoot through fields of laughter,
our hands reaching for stars
that we believed only we could touch.

The world felt
smaller
when you stood beside me,
and time dared not move
when we whispered dreams
into the wind.

I thought forever lived in your eyes.
I never knew how fragile infinity could be.

Sonnet: "In the Glow of What We Were"

We danced beneath the moon's forgiving light,
Our hearts are unbound, too wild to be contained.
Your laughter echoed softly through the night,
A love so bright, the world could not explain.

Your eyes, two oceans pulling me to shore,
Where dreams were real, and time would never end.
I craved your touch, I only longed for more,
My soul became your shadow, and you my best friend.

Yet fate, in envy, placed us in the sky,
Two stars that burned too close, then fell apart.
But even now, as distant as we lie,
Your memory still lingers in my heart.

For love that lived too boldly ever dies,
It hides within the tears that fill my eyes.

Haiku: "Shattered Bonds"

Hands that once held mine,
Now strangers in crowded streets.
Time forgets us both.

Narrative Poetry: "The Bridge We Burned"

We were young when we built that bridge,
Carved from midnight talks and promises
That felt too eternal to break.
You held my hand,
And I believed
We would never fall apart.

But time wears on everything,
Even the strongest of souls.
You grew quiet,
And I grew distant.
The space between us stretched,
Until words became wounds
And silence became safer than speaking.

I still remember the night we let the flames consume us.
Anger turned to ashes,
And all that remained
Was the bitter taste of goodbye.

I walk that bridge in my dreams sometimes,
Hoping to find you on the other side.
But you're never there,
Only the smoke of what we used to be.

"Before the Fall"

I remember how your voice softened when you spoke my name. How the world felt quieter when you were near. You made me believe that some souls are meant to find each other in every lifetime. We built dreams from stardust and promises, never thinking the sky would someday let us fall.

"I Was Yours Before I Knew Myself"

I met you in a moment
when my heart was still learning how to bloom.
You traced sunlight on my skin,
and I let you in too soon.

We laughed in colours
the world had never seen,
And I swore I would keep you love.

Letter: "When Love Was Still Ours"

Dear You,

I think I loved you too deeply to notice the cracks forming between us.

I was so lost in the warmth of your presence,
I never imagined you'd become a memory I'd have to learn to live with.

There was a time when your laughter felt like home,
when your eyes held every version of me that I was afraid to be.
And I swear,
I would have stayed there forever
if forever had stayed with us.

I wonder if you ever miss the way we felt
before everything turned into distance.

I still carry the version of you that loved me.
And maybe that's where I went wrong —
Holding on to something
that was already slipping away.

We Fell Apart, And I Wrote About It.

Section II: The Falling Apart (Where Everything We Built Collapsed)

12   We Fell Apart, And I Wrote About It.

The Silence Between Us"

I felt you slipping
long before you let go.

Your words turned cold
Your eyes
distant
and I drowned in the silence
that filled the space between us.

I tried to hold on,
but love is heavy
when only one heart is carrying it

Sonnet: "The Day You Stopped Saying My Name"

Your voice once wrapped me softly in the night,
 But now it cuts through shadows, cold and bare.
 Your eyes, once filled with warmth and burning light,
 Now turn away, pretending I'm not there.

I reach for you, but you have turned to stone,
 A heart that beat for me now beats for none.
 I stand in ruins, left to grieve alone,
 While you move on as if we'd just begun.

How cruel is love, that it can fade away,
 Yet leave the soul to ache another day.

Haiku: "Falling Out of Us"

Hands that used to hold
Now tremble when reaching out.
Love dies quietly.

Prose Poetry: "The Night We Broke Without Words"

You sat across from me, and I knew it was over before you said a thing. The air between us felt heavy, thick with everything we never dared to speak. I wanted to ask if you still loved me, but I was too afraid of the answer. So, I let the silence speak for both of us. And that's how we ended—

Not with anger.

Not with goodbye.

But with quiet surrender.

Lyrical Poetry: "You Let Me Go So Easily"

Was I that easy to forget?
Did my love leave no trace on your skin?
Tell me, when you hear my name,
Does it sound like something you've never been in?

I held your heart like fragile glass,
But you let mine slip through your hands.
Now I'm drowning in the memories
Of a love I'll never understand.

Narrative poetry: "The Stranger You Became"

I saw it first in your eyes,
the way you looked at me
like I was something you once wanted
but now I regret keeping.

We used to be everything—
Laughter on rainy nights,
Kisses that burned through skin,
Hands that never let go.

But slowly,
I became invisible to you,
like the spaces between words
that no one ever reads.

I watched you slip away,
while I stood still,
begging time to take me back
to when we were whole.

Letter: "The Breaking That Became Me"

Dear You,

I kept searching for you in places you never planned to stay.

I begged the universe for signs,
 for reasons,
 for something that would make the ending hurt a little less.

But all I found was silence.

And in that silence,
 I realized...

You weren't mine to keep.
 Maybe you never were.

Losing you felt like losing pieces of myself,
 until one day,
 I looked in the mirror
 and saw someone who survived you.

I'm not angry anymore.
 I'm not waiting either.

I'm just learning how to live
 without reaching for a hand
 that let go of me a long time ago.

We Fell Apart, And I Wrote About It.

Section III: The Aftermath (Where I Learned To Survive)

We Fell Apart, And I Wrote About It.

"I Loved You and I Survived"

I woke up one morning
 and your name didn't burn my throat.

I stood in front of the mirror
 and saw someone
 who was learning to live
 without the weight of your memory.

You were my storm,
 but I am the sky
 that survived you.

Sonnet - "What Healing Sounds Like"

No longer do your whispers fill my head,
Nor do your ghosts lie heavy on my chest.
I've buried every word you left unsaid,
And let my shattered heart be put to rest.

The night no longer calls me back to you,
The dawn has kissed my skin with something new.
I wear my wounds like armor, strong and true,
For broken hearts can bloom when pain is through.

You were the fire that burned me to the ground,
Yet from the ashes, I have now been found.

Haiku: "I Let You Go"

I released your name,
Watched it float into the wind.
I breathed for the first time.

Prose Poetry: "The Day I Stopped Waiting for You"

I stopped checking my phone for your name. Stopped walking past the places where we used to meet. I no longer search for your face in crowded streets or hope the universe will bring you back to me.

I realized I was holding onto a version of you that no longer existed. And maybe, I was holding onto a version of myself that only knew how to love you.

So, I let us go.

Lyrical Poetry: "I Loved, I Lost, I Grew"

I loved you like the sea loves the shore,
Endless, wild, and wanting more.

But you drifted away with the tide,
And I learned to find the strength inside.

Now I bloom where your shadow fades,
In places where my heart wasn't afraid.
I lost you,
But I found me.

Narrative Poetry: "The Version of Me That No Longer Loves You"

There was a time I thought I couldn't breathe without you.
A time when your absence felt like my own body betraying me.

But slowly,
I learned how to exist in the spaces you left behind.
I wrote poems you would never read,
and danced in rooms you'd never enter.

I became someone
who no longer waits for your return,
but instead,
writes stories about how beautifully I survived your leaving.

Final Letter: "To The Version of Me That Survived"

Dear Me,

You thought this heartbreak would destroy you.
And for a while, it did.

You wrote about them in every poem,
drowned in memories,
and held onto ghosts
that were never meant to stay.

But look at you now.

You turned your pain into poetry,
 your grief into art,
 and your heartbreak into something beautiful.

You loved them deeply,
 but you saved yourself.

And maybe...
 that's the kind of love
 that was always meant to last.

- Me

Like stars that shine their fiercest just before fading into the night, they were never built to last—yet somehow, they always did. Fate tried to break them, time challenged their bond, and life pulled them down separate roads. But no matter the distance or the silence, they always found their way back to each other. It was as though the universe refused to let them stay apart, as if some unseen force tugged at their souls, again and again, no matter the heartbreak, the destruction, or the promises made in anger.

Because some hearts—especially the ones that have known loss, tasted love, and bled from its absence—aren't ruled by coincidence. They're bound by something timeless, something written not just in moments, but in the spaces between them. And so, even when they shattered, even when they swore it was the end, their story remained—etched in the silences, in the ruins, in the memory of everything they were, and everything they could never quite become.

About the Author

Disha Agarwal

Disha Agarwal writes to remember, and sometimes, to forget. A collector of moments and emotions, her work blends free verse, lyrical fragments, and narrative poetry to explore the fragile threads of love, loss, and memory. When she's not writing, she's revisiting old memories, listening to songs that hurt a little, or finding poetry in the quietest corners of life.

We Fell Apart, And I Wrote About It is her debut—a love letter to the ones who stayed, the ones who left, and the versions of ourselves we leave behind.

www.ingramcontent.com/pod-product-compliance
Lightning Source LLC
LaVergne TN
LVHW041600070526
838199LV00046B/2073